CAROLINE PITCHER took her degree in English and European Literature at Warwick University and later became a primary school teacher in east London. Her previous books include *The Sue Tribe* and *On the Wire* (both Blackie) and *Gerald and the Pelican* (Yearling). Her first title for Frances Lincoln was *The Snow Whale*, which was chosen as one of *Child Education's* Best Books of 1996 and shortlisted for the 1997 Children's Book Award. It was followed by *The Time of the Lion*. Caroline lives in Belper, Derbyshire with her two children.

JACKIE MORRIS grew up in the Cotswolds and studied illustration at Bath Academy. *Lord of the Dance* (Lion), *Grandmother's Song* and Susan Summers' *The Greatest Gift* (both Barefoot), Anita Ganeri's *Journeys Through Dreamtime* (Macdonald Young Books) and Ted Hughes' *How the Whale Became* (Faber) are some of her most recent books. Her first two collaborations with Caroline Pitcher for Frances Lincoln were on *The Snow Whale* and *The Time of the Lion* – whose watercolour illustrations were acclaimed by *Books for Keeps* for their "strength and majesty". Jackie lives in West Wales with her husband and two children.

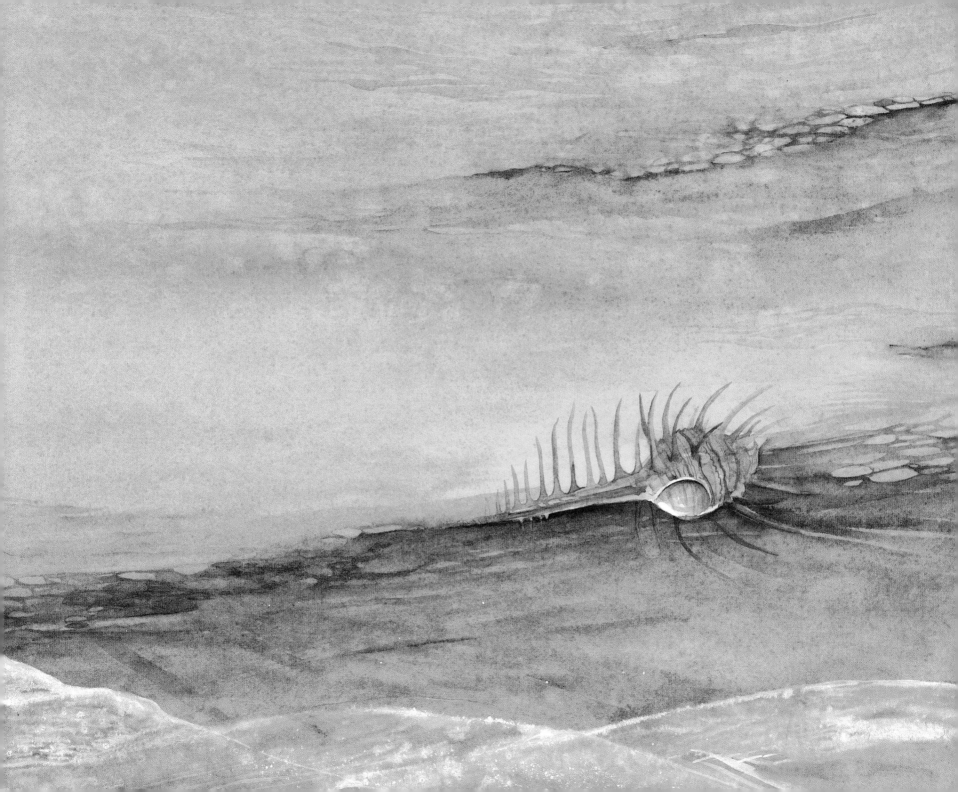

For dear Esther, granny to Lauren and Max – C.P.
For Lis Cousens, with love – J.M.

This is a traditional Chilean folk tale, reproduced
in *Folk Tales from Chile* by Brenda Hughes,
(George G. Harrap & Co. Ltd, 1962)

Mariana and the Merchild copyright © Frances Lincoln Limited 2000
Text copyright © Caroline Pitcher 2000
Illustrations copyright © Jackie Morris 2000

First published in Great Britain in 2000 by
Frances Lincoln Limited, 4 Torriano Mews
Torriano Avenue, London NW5 2RZ

First paperback edition 2001

British Library Cataloguing in Publication Data
available on request

ISBN hardback 0-7112-1465-4
ISBN paperback 0-7112-1464-6

Printed in Hong Kong
1 3 5 7 9 8 6 4 2

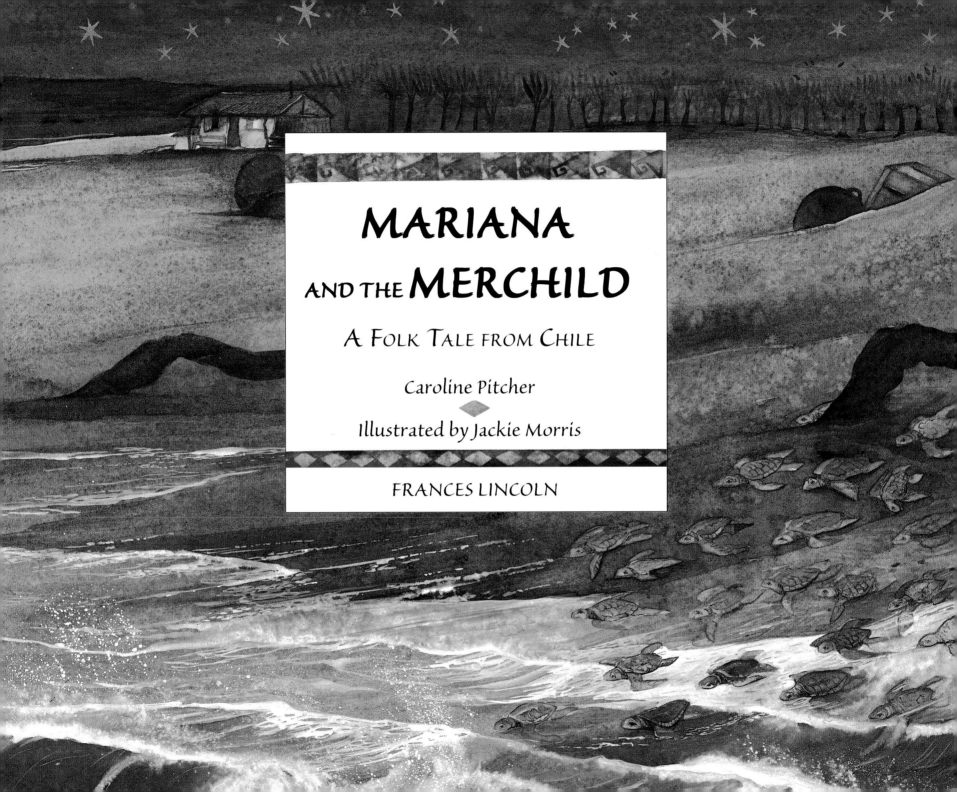

MARIANA
AND THE MERCHILD

A FOLK TALE FROM CHILE

Caroline Pitcher

Illustrated by Jackie Morris

FRANCES LINCOLN

An old woman lived alone in a hut by the sea. Her name was Mariana.

The waves boomed and sucked pebbles and shells from the shore. Mariana loved to listen to its music. The sea was like a mother to her. It brought her fish to eat, wood to burn and music to listen to. But sometimes it filled her with fear. You see, deep in the sea caves and forests there hid hungry sea-wolves, waiting for a storm.

Whenever Mariana walked on the shore, the village children crept along after her, pulling faces. Mariana longed for the children to be her friends, but if she turned round, they ran!

One day a storm came, and it was terrible! The winds tore at the hut and tugged at the roof. The sea-wolves threw back their heads and howled, and then out they came. All night they prowled along the shore, howling and baying in the wind and rain. All night Mariana trembled in the corner of her ramshackle hut, with her hands clapped tight over her ears.

Towards dawn, the winds tired and the sea-wolves crept back into their underwater caves. Mariana tiptoed to the door, opened it and looked out. The storm had blown the sky clear of clouds and the sunlight dazzled her, bright as a mirror burst into a million pieces.

She stood in the warm sunlight to soothe her rickety-rackety bones. The sea surged as if a volcano had thrown out jewels of turquoise and indigo, aquamarine and emerald.

"The sea has brought me fish and wood!" she said. "There's plenty here – enough to cook food for the children, if they would let me."

Mariana peered into a rock pool. It was as clear as glass, and full of treasures brought by the sea. She saw ruby anemones, a shell like a sunburst, a silver sea horse and a golden starfish. In the middle, half-hidden by seaweed, lay a crab as fine as a shield.

"There's enough crab here to feed me all week!" cried Mariana. She put the crab into her basket, then collected seaweed and driftwood for her fire.

She struggled back to her hut and put her basket on the table. When she lifted the seaweed, she saw that the crab had split in two.

"Why, what's this?" cried Mariana.

It was a baby girl, with hair the colour of the setting sun, and skin that gleamed like a rosy pearl, and a fish's tail with scales of silver.

"Look what the sea has brought me!" cried Mariana. And at once she loved that baby more than she had ever loved anything.

She carried the baby in its crab-shell cradle to the village, and laid her in the Wise Woman's arms.

For a long time the Wise Woman said nothing. Then she said, "This is a Merbaby. Her mother hid her in the crab shell to keep her safe from the sea-wolves."

"Then I must let the mother know she is safe," said Mariana. "Who *is* her mother?"

"A Sea Spirit," said the Wise Woman. "So take care, Mariana. Put the Merbaby safely on a rock out of reach of the sea-wolves, and hide away to watch."

Mariana went back to the shore and set the crab shell high on a rock.

She smiled down at the Merbaby and said, "*You're* not afraid of me, are you?" And the Merbaby smiled back.

Mariana hid herself away and waited. She was just about to fall asleep in the sun when she heard someone singing, but not words from this world.

Seven great waves came rolling into shore, waves of crimson and rose and gold, and on the seventh wave rode the Sea Spirit. She was tall as a mast. Her hair flamed red and her skin shone as if polished by the sun with mother-of-pearl. All the colours of the rainbow shimmered in her fish's tail. Her opal eyes, full of fire, lit upon the crab shell cradle.

The Sea Spirit picked up her Merbaby and sang a lullaby not of this world. Her voice sighed like the far-away pull of the sea.

"I didn't mean to steal your baby!" cried Mariana. "I thought the sea had brought her for me!"

The Sea Spirit looked at Mariana. Her eyes flickered, no colour and every colour. She said, "The sea *did* bring her for you, Mariana. I hid her inside the shell to keep her from the sea-wolves, but the storm swept the cradle away. You have saved her life. Look after her for me now, until the seas lie calm. I will come every day to feed her and teach her how to swim."

So Mariana and the Merchild lived together in the ramshackle hut, safe from the restless sea. It was the happiest time of the old woman's life.

The Merchild grew stronger and her hair grew longer, burnished red as the setting sun. She liked to lie in the shallow waves and watch the shells open and close like mouths. She laughed as she watched the village children running along the shore after the sea-birds, or jumping from rock to rock. They peeped over the rocks at Mariana, and no longer ran away when she smiled at them.

The Merchild liked to watch Mariana's fire spangling her tail with pink and vermilion.

The Merchild learnt to speak the words of our world. When she sang, her voice was like the echo of the sea inside a shell. Mariana loved her so!

Each day the Sea Spirit rode in on the seventh wave. She fed the Merchild and taught her to swim in the sheltered rock pool, and then further out to sea.

"Dear Merchild!" whispered Mariana. "I dread the time when you must return to the sea." And she thought to herself, "If I kept the Merchild shut in the hut, the Sea Spirit could not take her from me." Then she thought, "No. The Merchild is from the sea. I must let her return, even though I will be alone again."

Mariana went back to her hut, where the Merchild was making necklaces of shells for the village children. She looked up and smiled, and Mariana thought her heart would melt.

"Shall I cook you something to eat, children?" asked Mariana.

They looked at each other. Then, "Yes please!" they said.

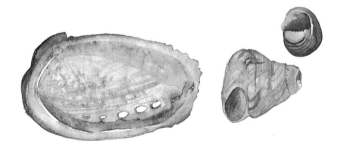

At last came the morning Mariana was dreading.

The Sea Spirit sang, "My child can swim now and it is time to take her home. The sea is calm and the sea-wolves cannot catch her. But we will never forget you, Mariana."

And she took her Merchild on her back, far far out to sea, while Mariana stood with tears streaming down her face.

The children stole up behind Mariana. They took her hands and comforted her.

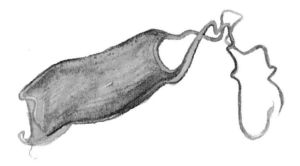

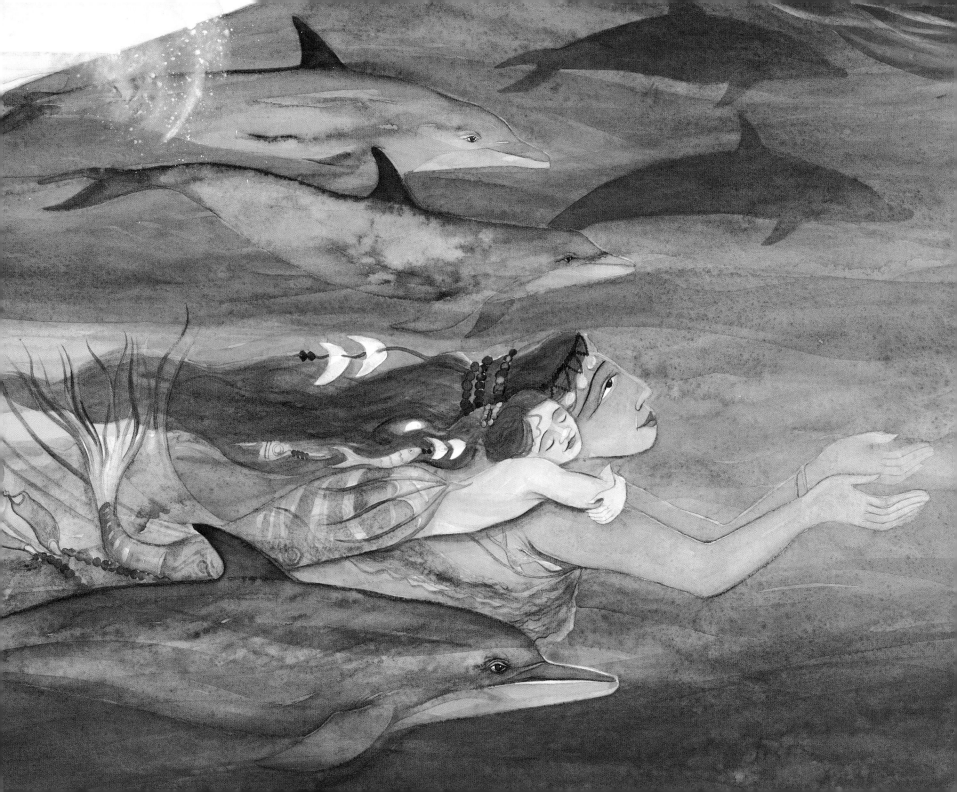

But the Merchild had not gone forever. Each morning she leapt from the waves to greet Mariana. Every day she gave her a lustrous pearl from the sea-bed. The Sea Spirit sent in waves brimful of fish, and the rock pools teemed with shrimps and crabs and seaweed. When there was a storm, the sea-wolves still howled, but Mariana was no longer afraid of them.

The children helped Mariana to carry her wood and food home, and now they always stayed for tea.

"Don't be sad, Mariana," they said. "The Sea Spirit and her child will never forget you. Nor will we."

And they never did.

OTHER PICTURE BOOKS IN PAPERBACK
FROM FRANCES LINCOLN

THE TIME OF THE LION

Caroline Pitcher

Illustrated by Jackie Morris

At night-time, when Joseph hears a Lion's roar, he decides to go and meet the Lion.
He sleeps beside him, meets his brave Lioness and watches the cubs play, learning that
danger is not always where you think. Then one day traders come looking for lion cubs ...

Suitable for National Curriculum English - Reading, Key Stages 1 and 2
Scottish Guidelines English Language - Reading, Level C

ISBN 0-7112-1338-0 £5.99

THE SNOW WHALE

Caroline Pitcher

Illustrated by Jackie Morris

One November morning, when the hills are hump-backed with snow,
Laurie and Leo decide to build a snow whale. As they shovel and pat and polish to
bring the snow whale out of the hill, the whale gradually takes on a life of its own.
Selected for Child Education's Best Books of 1996

Suitable for National Curriculum English - Reading, Key Stage 1
Scottish Guidelines English Language - Reading, Levels A and B

ISBN 0-7112-1093-4 £4.99

Frances Lincoln titles are available from all good bookshops.

Prices are correct at time of publication, but may be subject to change.